A Note to Parents & Teachers—

Welcome to We Can Readers from Xist Publishing! These books are designed to inspire discovery and delight in the youngest readers. Each short book features very simple sentences with visual cues to get kids reading for the first time.

You can help each child develop a lifetime love of reading right from the very start. Here are some ways to help a beginning reader get going:

- Read the book aloud as a first introduction
- Run your fingers below the words as you read each line
- Give the child the chance to finish the sentences or read repeating words while you read the rest.
- Encourage the child to read aloud every day!

Published proudly in the State of Texas, USA by Xist Publishing
www.xistpublishing.com
24200 Southwest Freeway Suite 402- 290 Rosenberg, TX 77471

eISBN: 978-1-5324-2995-8
Saddle Stitch ISBN: 978-1-5324-3020-6
Perfect Bound ISBN: 978-1-5324-4116-5
Hardcover ISBN: 978-1-5324-3530-0

Bandit Plays

Brenda Ponnay

xist Publishing

Bandit plays with the mouse.

The mouse goes up.

Bandit plays with
the light.

The light goes over.

Bandit plays with the string.

The string goes around.

Bandit plays with
the cup.

The cup goes down.

Bandit plays with the dog.

The dog goes back.

11

Bandit plays
with me.

Things to do next!

Write a Sentence

Bandit plays with_____.

Drawing

Draw something for Bandit
to play with.

Sharing

Talk to your classmates about how you
play with animals.

WORD LIST

at	my
Bandit	nap
bed	naps
day	night
does	not
funny	places
he	sunshine
I	the
in	to
it	too
like	under
likes	when
me	with

WE CAN
READERS